Boing-Boing

THE BIONIC CAT
AND THE JEWEL THIEF

Boing-Boing
THE BIONIC CAT
AND THE JEWEL THIEF

Written by Larry L. Hench
Illustrations by Ruth Denise Lear

Published by The Can of Worms Kids Press

1 3 5 7 9 10 8 6 4 2

First published in the UK in 2004 by
Can of Worms Kids Press
2 Peacock Yard
London SE17 3LH
United Kingdom

Telephone: +44 (0)845 123 3971
E-mail: info@canofwormspress.co.uk
Web site: www.canofwormspress.co.uk

Copyright © Can of Worms Enterprises Ltd 2004
Text Copyright © Larry L. Hench

First published in hardback by the American Ceramic Society 2001
ISBN: 1-57498-129-3

Printed and bound in Italy
Cover design – Alison Eddy
Text design – Shona O'Connor, Robert Whitaker
Producer – Can of Worms Design Group

A CIP catalogue record for this book is available from the British
Library

ISBN: 1-904872-01-8

For Daniel and Jessica

Professor George says...

Dear Readers

When Larry Hench became a grandfather, he started looking for books to read to his grandchildren that taught science concepts in a fun and interesting way, without talking down, through stories that were realistic—not fairytale-like. He couldn't find them; he was also dismayed to see scientists, professors, and engineers portrayed as evil, nutty, nerdy, absent-minded, etc...not as real, caring, helpful human beings. Larry wanted children to see the excitement and process of science, and scientists and engineers as trustworthy, interesting, and fun people. So he decided to write his own stories to accomplish these goals. Enter Boing-Boing!

Parents and Teachers: While these books have been written for enjoyment they have also been adopted by schools to help teach children aged seven and up about science and technology. In the Boing-Boing the Bionic Cat series the general synopsis of the books is as follows: Daniel, who loves cats but is allergic to them, is delighted when his inventive neighbour Professor George—that's me, an engineer— builds him a bionic cat with fibre-optic fur, computer-controlled joints, electronic eyes, and ceramic-sensor whiskers. It's just like a real cat, but Daniel is not allergic to it! With each succeeding adventure I add new technological features to Boing-Boing. Everything that I make Boing-Boing do in this book can be done at home or at school.

Glossary: Throughout the book you will find some words highlighted in bold. These words may be difficult for some readers to understand, so at the end of this book you will find a glossary explaining their meanings.

If you have any questions about Boing-Boing please do not hesitate to write to me by e-mail: professor.george@boing-boing.org or by post: Professor George, c/o Can of Worms Press, 2 Peacock Yard, London SE17 3LH, United Kingdom.

Contents

Bionic Cat

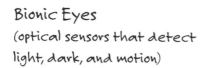

Bionic Eyes
(optical sensors that detect light, dark, and motion)

Bionic Whiskers
(piezoelectric ceramics on the end of metallic conductors that convert heat, pressure, and mechanical deflection into electrical signals)

Computer
(small, powerful, programmable microprocessor that converts electrical signals from sensors to control bionic legs, tail, head, and voice box)

Bionic Tail
(four multi-axial joints that enable tail to move in all directions under computer control)

Design Features

Fibre-Optic Fur
(optical glass fibre, covering over all surfaces, that transmits sunlight through the fibres to photoelectric cells that charge the batteries)

Bionic Voice Box
(programmable voice simulator activated by sensors embedded in the fibre-optic fur; controlled by the computer)

Bionic Tail Sensor
(piezoelectric ceramic sensor in tail joint that sends signals to the computer and voice simulator to generate a ROAR with the loudness increasing as pressure on the sensor increases)

Batteries
(6 rechargeable 9-volt batteries that provide power to the computer, the bionic eyes, tail, legs, head, and ceramic heating elements)

Bionic Legs
(4 legs with 3 multi-axial joints per leg connected to small motors controlled by the computer)

Chapter One

Daniel was sitting on his front porch waiting for Professor George to come home from the university. It was getting late and Daniel said to himself, "Poor Professor George, he must be working late again. He does work hard. I'll just have to wait until tomorrow to ask him." Daniel's mum had come to the door and overheard. "What do you want to ask Professor George, Dan?" she asked. "Oh nothing," he replied. Daniel did not want his mother to know what was bothering him.

"Well it's about time to eat. Come in and wash your hands, Dan."

"Okay Mum," Daniel answered.

Just then, he saw his friend coming round the corner. "Professor George! Professor George!" Daniel shouted as he jumped up to meet him.

"Hello Daniel," said Professor George. "How are you? Why are you so excited?"

"It's Boing-Boing. Something has happened to him. Can you look at him, please?" asked Daniel, holding out his bionic cat to the professor.

"Of course," answered Professor George as he took the **bionic** cat.

"I don't see anything unusual," Professor George said as he looked at the cat. Everything appeared to be in place. The bionic cat's shiny fur sparkled in the sunlight. The fur was made of very fine glass fibres that carry sunlight to special **solar cells** inside the cat where the sunlight is converted to energy that charges Boing-Boing's **batteries**.

His special whiskers were in good shape too. The bionic cat's whiskers, made of very thin wires with special **ceramic sensors** on the ends, were important because they kept Boing-Boing out of

danger. Some of the sensors can feel objects in Boing-Boing's way and let him know to move around them using his battery-driven legs. Other sensor's on the whiskers detect heat or cold and warn the cat of danger.

Next, Professor George looked into the bionic cat's eyes that glowed with a soft yellow light. These bionic eyes were connected to a very small **computer** in the cat's belly. The computer used very little power so the cat can sit still for hours and hours without moving and still be alert and full of energy.

Professor George had made the bionic cat to be just like a real cat, and Daniel loved Boing-Boing very much.

"What's wrong with Boing-Boing, Dan?" asked the professor.

Daniel answered, "Boing-Boing has stopped purring when I pet him.

"See – when I stroke him like this, nothing happens."

Daniel liked to hold Boing-Boing. The

bionic cat was slightly warm and his **fibre-optic** fur was shiny. When the fur was stroked, the cat would make a gentle "purr-purr" sound.

Professor George listened closely to the bionic cat. "You're right, Dan," he said. "There's no sound at all when you pet him. Maybe a wire connecting his **voice box** to the computer has come loose."

"I don't think that's the problem, Professor George," responded Daniel. "Just listen."

He rubbed his cat's nose and the bionic cat quickly said, "Boing-Boing!" He did it again and the cat repeated, "Boing-Boing!"

Professor George laughed. "I guess you're right, Dan. There's nothing wrong with his voice box or the wiring." He added, "I am still surprised when I hear him say 'Boing-Boing' instead of 'meow-meow' like cats should. I don't know how I made that mistake when I **programmed** the computer."

"Professor George," said Daniel. "You shouldn't be unhappy because you made a mistake. Boing-Boing is the only cat in the world that says its own name. Boing-Boing is really special. I'm glad he doesn't 'meow-meow' like everyone else's cats."

"Well, I'm happy that you like it so much, Dan. But it is still a little frustrating to me," sighed Professor George.

"Do you think you can fix Boing-Boing so he can purr again?" asked Daniel.

"I'll try," replied Professor George as he took the bionic cat from Daniel.

"Promise you won't stop Boing-Boing from saying his name!" Daniel called out as his friend walked away.

"I promise," said Professor George, already wondering what was wrong with the cat.

After dinner Professor George said to his wife, "Honey, I 'm going downstairs to my workshop for a little while to see if I can fix Boing-Boing for Dan."

"All right," she answered. "Just make sure you don't lose track of time. Promise you won't stay down there all night like you did when you built Boing-Boing. You have an early class in the morning."

"I promise," he answered as he started down the steps.

Chapter Two

Professor George walked down to his basement workshop. It was a very special workshop – a small version of the bioengineering research lab that he directed at the university.

On his workbench were many tools and special **ceramic** parts. He also had lots of electronic equipment and a powerful computer, nicknamed Supie, which was connected to the big **super computer** at the university.

Professor George turned on his computer, typed in his passwords and said, partly to himself and partly to the computer, "Well, Supie, let's see what's wrong with Boing-Boing."

He unscrewed the small plate in the bionic cat's belly and opened the

compartment containing the cat's little computer. Next, he attached some wires from his computer to the bionic cat.

"OK, Supie," he muttered. "Show me what's wrong with this little guy."

The computer screen lit up with a coloured display of the wiring inside

Boing-Boing.

Professor George used the mouse connected to the computer to follow the circuit controlling the **voice simulator**.

"Hey, isn't that funny," he chuckled to himself. "I'm using a mouse to fix a cat! Dan will get a real laugh at that when I tell him tomorrow.

"There it is!" exclaimed Professor George, peering closely at the computer screen. "A piece of dust is causing a short between two wires. That's why you're not purring, little fellow. No problem, I can fix you in no time at all."

After removing the dust with a pair of tweezers, Professor George said to himself, "Aha, I have an idea. I'll add a nice surprise to Boing-Boing for Dan."

So he began typing some changes into the computer program that controlled Boing-Boing's voice simulator.

Professor George finished and put

Boing-Boing on the floor. "There! You're even more special now. Let's see how your new talent works."

He tested the change and laughed at the results.

"Yes, indeed. Boing-Boing, you will really give Dan a big surprise tomorrow. Now, I must look at tomorrow's lecture notes and then to bed."

Chapter Three

The next evening Daniel was waiting eagerly on his front steps. "Professor George! Professor George!" he called when he saw his friend. "Is Boing-Boing okay?"

"He sure is," answered Professor George. "Come, and I'll show you. In fact, he's even better than before."

"Oh, no!" responded Daniel. "You didn't stop him saying 'Boing-Boing' did you?"

"Of course not, Dan," said Professor George. "Remember, I promised you I wouldn't."

"Yes," said Daniel. "I'm sorry."

Professor George took Daniel down to his workshop.

Daniel picked up the bionic cat and switched him on. He stroked the fibre-optic fur and heard a very pleasant "purr-purr."

"Great," said Daniel. Then he rubbed the bionic cat's nose and heard "Boing-Boing, Boing-Boing."

"Super!" Daniel exclaimed. "You're right, Professor George. He's as good as new."

"Wrong, " replied the professor. "He's better than new. Here, I'll show you."

Professor George put the bionic cat on the floor. The cat's tail slowly switched back and forth.

"Watch, Dan," he said. "After a few minutes the tail will stop since the cat is not moving."

"That's neat!" said Daniel.

"The best is yet to come," responded Professor George. "Squeeze Boing-Boing's tail very gently and see what happens."

Daniel ever so gently squeezed his cat's tail and then jumped back with a fright as Boing-Boing let out a great big "ROAR!"

"WOW!" shouted Daniel. "How did he do that?"

Professor George laughed and said, "I put a new ceramic **sensor** in Boing-Boing's tail and programmed another set of commands to his voice simulator, Dan.

"Squeeze his tail a little bit harder – not too hard though! You don't want to break

his fibre-optic fur."

Daniel very carefully squeezed the tail,
this time a little bit harder.

He jumped back again as Boing-Boing

let out an even louder "R.O.A̶R̶!̶!̶"

"WOW!" Daniel shouted again. "This is unbelievable. Boing-Boing sounds just like the lion I saw in the Zoo. He is awesome. He is really scary!"

"You need to be careful, Dan, about using this new talent of Boing-Boing's," cautioned Professor George. "You shouldn't frighten people just for fun. But it can be useful if you or your cat is in danger."

"I'll say," responded Daniel. "His roar would surprise anyone, anytime. Thanks a lot Professor George. You do invent some clever things. I'll see you tomorrow."

Chapter Four

The next morning was Saturday, Daniel woke up, yawned, and looked at Boing-Boing sitting on the windowsill, soaking up the sunshine.

He picked up his bionic cat and gently stroked his fur. Boing-Boing said, "purrr-purrr."

"Great!" thought Daniel. "You're still okay."

He then very, very gently squeezed his bionic cat's tail. "ROAR!" responded the cat, sounding just like a fierce lion.

Daniel was glad he had only squeezed the tail a little bit. He did not want his mother to be alarmed.

"Wow! If I gave your tail a really hard squeeze, your roar could be heard all the way to Professor George's house," thought Daniel. "I really need to remember to be careful."

After breakfast Daniel's mother asked, "Dan, do you still want to go to the museum today?"

"Yes!" he replied. "I've been waiting all week."

"Are you certain that you can get there and back by yourself?" asked his mother.

"Of course I can," said Daniel. "You've taken me there many times. I could do it in my sleep."

"All right, you can go on your own this time," his mother said. "But be sure to call if you get lost, and be home by three o'clock. No later or I'll worry."

"Okay, Mummy, I promise," replied Daniel as he ran from the room.

When Daniel got to his room he took his bionic cat from the windowsill and asked, "Boing-Boing, would you like to go to the museum with me?

"Bye, Mummy," he called out as he left the house with his bionic cat. "I'll be home by three o'clock."

A few blocks away, Daniel caught the bus that took him to the Natural History Museum. As he rode along, he watched out the window and petted Boing-Boing. His bionic cat felt nice and warm and purred very happily.

At the museum, Daniel bounded up
three flights of steps. The Natural History
Museum was a very large building that
used to frighten Daniel when he was little.
The twin towers seemed to reach to the sky
and the stone animal carvings all around
the building scared him. Now, though, the

museum was one of his favourite places. Daniel went through the large wooden doors and entered the huge central hall.

He turned left and looked up. High, high above him towered the skeleton of a dinosaur. It was huge, as tall as a four-storey building. Daniel stopped to read the sign. "I remember this, it is a Diplodocus," he told Boing-Boing. "I saw these on TV, but this real skeleton is much more impressive.

"This dinosaur was just about the largest animal to have walked on earth, and it ate hundreds of pounds of plants every day."

Nearby was Tyrannosaurus Rex, the fiercest dinosaur of them all. It had the biggest teeth and the strongest jaws, and was believed to be a mean, mad eating-machine that preyed on the dinosaurs that ate plants.

"T-Rex, you sure are huge," said Daniel,

as he looked up at the 35-foot high reconstructed dinosaur. "Your teeth are as big as my cat. I'm glad you're not alive now. You could eat me up in one bite."

Daniel walked all around T-Rex, taking one last look at him. He was imagining what life was like millions of years ago.

As he turned to go on, Daniel clutched his bag tightly. Then he jumped with fright. He thought he had seen T-Rex look down at him and roar.

Daniel clutched his bag even tighter. This time, he was certain he heard a frightening roar coming from the huge dinosaur.

Daniel's eyes got very big. He turned pale. His teeth started to chatter. He tried to run but he couldn't. His legs would not move a step. His feet felt like they were

glued to the ground. He began to tremble and clutched his bag even tighter. Again he heard an even louder "ROARRR!"

He was sure the T-Rex was going to pick him up and eat him. He yelled, "Help! Help! Someone, help!"

A museum guard came running. "What's the matter young man?" he asked. "What's wrong?"

"I'm s-s-so glad to see you. I thought for s-s-sure I s-s-saw that huge dinosaur m-m-move and r-r-roar at me," stammered Daniel.

"Well, I agree he does look real," answered the guard. "But I assure you that he has not moved or roared for as long as I can remember."

"But I heard him roar," pleaded Daniel. "I really did."

"It must have been your imagination.

Tyrannosaurus Rex was alive about 65 million years ago. He has not roared for a long, long time, and he's just a skeleton now, like all the others you see here.

"OK? Have you seen the whales yet? They won't frighten you. Why don't you run along now?"

"Thanks a lot," replied Daniel. "I guess it must have been my imagination. But, it sure sounded like a real roar. I'll go see the whales next. Thanks, again. Bye."

Chapter Five

Daniel went quickly into the hall nearby, called Whale Hall.

"WOW!" he exclaimed. "I'd forgotten just how big whales are."

He was looking at both the skeleton and the recreation of a blue whale that filled the centre of the hall. The sign said:

> **WHALES are mammals. They are not fishes even though they look similar to fishes. The blue whale is the largest mammal to have ever lived on earth. It can be more than 100 feet long.**

Daniel, remembering another museum he had visited, said "Mister whale, guess what? You're even bigger than a train engine. I wonder how many carloads of fish you can pull?"

The next sign read:

> **WHALES**, ultimately, get their energy from sunlight. Small plants, called plankton convert the sunlight. Very small shrimp-like animals, called krill eat the plankton, and the whales eat the krill. They eat tons of krill, roaming the seas of the world in search of food.

"WOW!" he thought. "Boing-Boing and a blue whale have something in common – their energy comes from the sun! Boing-Boing gets his energy from the sunlight that travels through his fibre-optic fur, converts to electricity, and charges the batteries. And the blue whale gets energy from the sun, but by eating krill." Daniel remarked, "nature is fantastic."

The next sign Daniel and Boing-Boing saw told them:

BLUE WHALE

WHALES breathe air to live.
When a whale comes to the surface to
spout, it is exhaling carbon dioxide.
The whale then breathes in air
containing oxygen before it dives.

"That is really cool," said Daniel. "Whales breathe in air to live just like I do! That is a big difference between Boing-Boing and this big blue whale," concluded Daniel. "Boing-Boing doesn't breathe in oxygen or breathe out carbon dioxide. He lives without breathing at all. That's another reason he's a bionic cat instead of a real cat."

After a while Daniel grew tired of looking at the whales and went in the next room.

"Oh boy!" he said, "these are my favourites!"

He looked around and tried to decide which was best. He was surrounded by sharks, dozens of species of sharks.

There were little sharks, medium-sized sharks, and even the giant whale shark that can grow to 40 feet long.

"It's a good thing they are all stuffed," said Daniel. "I wouldn't like to have another scare like I did with T-Rex. I

wonder why I heard that roar?"

Then Daniel remembered. "Of course! I bet it was Boing-Boing."

So he clutched his bag a little harder. "R·O·A·R!" went the bag.

Daniel opened it and looked in. "Boing-Boing are you unhappy in there? How silly of me to have forgotten about your new talent. No wonder that museum guard thought I was a little crazy.

"How would you like to see some really neat fishes, Boing-Boing?" asked Daniel. "I bet a bionic cat likes fishes, even if you don't eat them like real cats do."

So Daniel showed Boing-Boing the various species of sharks. "See, there's a nurse shark, and a mako shark, and a tiger shark, and a hammerhead shark. WOW. Boing-Boing, look at the jaws of this great white shark. Its teeth are almost as big as those of T-Rex. I guess it is the T-Rex of the seas. I wonder if Professor George could make a bionic shark? That would be really exciting," said Daniel.

Chapter Six

Then Daniel asked, "How would you like to see some of your relatives, Boing-Boing?"

He gave the bag a small squeeze and Boing-Boing responded with a tiny "ROAR."

"Okay, let's go," he said as they went looking for the animals in the cat family.

"Here are your aunts, uncles, and cousins, Boing-Boing," said Daniel. "WOW! They are really big."

He looked around the balcony of the central hall and saw a jaguar, a leopard, a lion, a tiger, and a cheetah. He also saw something very unusual.

"Look, Boing-Boing. Here's one of your ancestors from thousands of years ago – a saber-toothed tiger. It is extinct; no more live anywhere on earth. WOW!

"Those incisor teeth are awesome! They are even bigger than those of the great white shark and T-Rex!"

Next, Daniel stopped in front of the lion. "The lion is called the king of the jungle, Boing-Boing. Can you imagine what a bionic lion would be like? I could ride it to and from school. The other kids would be even more surprised than when I took you to school for 'Show and Tell.' I'll ask Professor George if he can build a bionic lion."

Just then Daniel had another idea. "Boing-Boing, would you like to sit down next to your big aunts and uncles? I'd like to see how you look compared to these big cats."

So, Daniel took Boing-Boing out of his bag and set him down near a stuffed lion.

He stepped back to look at his cat and compare it with the huge wild cats.

Daniel forgot that his bionic cat was

turned on with nearly a full battery charge.

Boing-Boing's tail switched a few times, then he became still, his eyes glowing slightly.

Just then a museum guard came around the corner. It was the same guard who had helped Daniel earlier. "Well young man, I see that you are not frightened of the jungle cats. They are more fierce today than dinosaurs, you know."

"I know, sir. It was silly of me to be scared by T-Rex. It won't happen again," Daniel responded.

"You need to run on home now," instructed the guard. "It's closing time."

"Oh no!" cried Daniel. "I'll be in real trouble. I promised my mum I'd be home by three o'clock. She'll be really worried."

"It's much later than that," said the guard. "I'll tell you what will help. There's a phone nearby. You can give her a call and tell her not to worry."

"Thank you. Thank you very much," responded Daniel. "She will be ever so grateful."

Daniel went off quickly with the guard to make the call. He was so worried that he forgot all about Boing-Boing sitting quietly next to the lion.

It was only after Daniel was on the bus that he felt his bag and realised it was empty.

He turned cold all over. He knew right away that he had left Boing-Boing in the museum. A big tear rolled down his cheek. "What am I going to do?" he cried.

Chapter Seven

When Daniel arrived home he knew he was in big trouble. He had lots of explaining and apologising to do. "I'm sorry Mummy," he said sobbing. "I forgot all about the time. I really didn't mean to be bad. I was just so interested in everything that I forgot to look at the clock. Then, to make it even worse, I forgot Boing-Boing. Are you going to punish me?"

His mother replied, "Leaving your bionic cat in the museum overnight is creating your own punishment, Daniel. That's what often happens to people, even grown-ups. We do something we shouldn't and then suffer the consequences. This should be a real lesson to you about what happens when you are irresponsible."

"What will happen to Boing-Boing,

Mummy? Maybe the museum will throw him away by mistake!" pleaded Daniel.

"I doubt that, Daniel, but let's try to call anyway," suggested his mother.

After the phone rang many times, she finally said, "No luck. We'll just have to wait until the museum opens tomorrow and we'll go get him then."

Daniel went to bed that night very sad and very worried. He hoped that Boing-Boing would be okay all alone in the museum.

But Boing-Boing was not alone.

Late that night something very exciting happened, and Boing-Boing was right in the middle of it. In fact, what happened that night made Boing-Boing the most famous cat in the country.

It was about two o'clock in the morning. The museum was very quiet. All the cleaning crew had come and gone. Only one guard remained, and he was slowly making his rounds inspecting the museum's many rooms.

Slowly, ever so slowly, a door opened from a passageway between the Natural History Museum and the Geological Museum.

A man slipped through the door without making a sound.

He was dressed all in black – even his sneakers. He had a black mask covering everything but his eyes. He had a black stocking cap pulled down over his ears and he was carrying a large black bag. The bag was full and very heavy.

The man had been hiding in an old, forgotten storeroom in the basement of the Geological Museum. When everyone had gone, he disabled all the alarms. Then, one by one, he opened the jewel cases displayed in the museum and removed all of the very best **gems**.

He took **rubies**, **sapphires**, and emeralds. Then he took the biggest and best **diamonds**. The jewels, all very old and rare, were some of the best in the world. It would

be a terrible loss for the museum to have these precious gems stolen.

But the burglar's plans were not perfect and he was in trouble. A delivery truck blocked his escape. He tried the door. It opened two inches, just enough to get his arm through. He tried again and almost got his head stuck!

Then the man remembered a small fire escape from the balcony, with a narrow ladder leading down to the ground. All he had to do was get there without the guard discovering him.

He silently sneaked along the hallway to the stairs leading up to the balcony. He stopped and listened very carefully. All was silent. "So far, so good," he whispered to himself. "Nothing here . . . just a bunch of dead animals. They can't hurt me. It looks like I'm safe."

He looked around and saw gigantic dinosaurs nearby. "I'm sure glad they're dead," he whispered nervously.

Slowly, the thief worked his way up to the balcony. Once there, he stopped and looked around. The moon was shining through a skylight so he could see a little better here. But, there were also lots of very dark shadows.

59

"Wow," he muttered to himself as he saw the family of jungle cats. "I'm glad those creatures are dead, too. They're worse than any dinosaur."

The man looked at the door with its FIRE ESCAPE sign glowing red above it.

He stared toward the door, stepping very carefully through the exhibit of large, wild cats.

He never noticed the two eyes following him. They were glowing slightly yellow and saw the man very clearly, even in the dark.

The thief never saw the tail start to switch back and forth as he stepped around the huge lion.

He never saw his foot land, and he never saw it step right on top of the tail.

But, the burglar certainly did hear the result – "R̊O̊ʻIR̊R̊R̊!̊!̊"

Boing-Boing let out a roar that echoed back and forth across the huge hall.

The burglar's head was only inches

from the lion's teeth, and that's all he saw. Lots and lots of teeth. Big, sharp pointed teeth. And all of them meant just for him.

Well, what do you think the thief did? You're right. He did what anyone else would do. He screamed – loud and long.

He yelled "HELLLP!" so loudly that he drowned out Boing-Boing's roar. Then he turned and ran.

"LET ME OUT! Let me out! Let me out!" he yelled, as he scrambled down the steps with jewels flying out of his bag all the way. His foot slipped on a couple of big red rubies and he bounced down the rest of the steps.

BOOM! BOOM! BOOM! He landed at the bottom, right at the feet of the museum guard.

The guard was a fan of old movies and likes a good joke. He shone his flashlight on the thief and the light sparkled back at him from the bright red gems.

"Well, what do we have here? It looks like Dorothy and her ruby slippers.

"Well buddy, whoever you are, you sure missed the Yellow Brick Road and this sure ain't Kansas! But, you are goin' to need a wizard to get out of this fix!"

The guard quickly put handcuffs on the man, who kept pleading, "Don't let him eat me! Don't let him eat me!"

Chapter Eight

Later that morning Daniel and his mother arrived at the museum as it opened. Daniel asked the guard who was still there, "Excuse me sir, I left my bionic cat here yesterday. May I go look for him?"

"So young man, you're the one who left that mechanical cat here. I think you had better come with me."

Daniel and his mum followed the guard to the museum director's office. The director was there along with several reporters, three policemen, and a detective from Scotland Yard. They all looked very serious. Daniel felt very small indeed. He was very worried and became even more scared when the director stood up. Daniel had not expected this much trouble. "Oh-oh," he thought. "This is worse than T-Rex was yesterday."

"Young man, is this yours?" asked the director, pointing to Boing-Boing who was walking on his desk.

Daniel answered, "Yes sir, it's mine. Professor George made it for me."

"Do you know what your cat did last night?" the director asked.

"No," replied Daniel in a very small voice. "I hope it wasn't something bad."

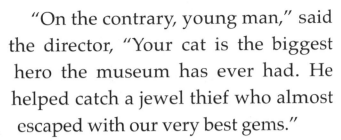

"On the contrary, young man," said the director, "Your cat is the biggest hero the museum has ever had. He helped catch a jewel thief who almost escaped with our very best gems."

"How did that happen?" asked Daniel.

The guard answered, "The thief apparently stepped on your cat as he was sneaking through the wild cat exhibit. We're not sure why, but he became very scared and then screamed for help. He ran away, slipped on the stairs, and fell right at my feet – the easiest arrest I've ever made. He pleaded with me to get him away from there. He was really scared."

Daniel thought for a minute and remembered where he had left Boing-Boing. He said, "I bet I know what happened – the thief thought that the huge lion was going to eat him."

"Why would he think that?" the

detective from Scotland Yard asked in disbelief.

"Here, I'll show you," replied Daniel as he reached over and picked up Boing-Boing. He took hold of his bionic cat's tail and gave it a really hard squeeze.

Boing-Boing responded instantly:

"ROARRR!!"

Everyone in the room jumped back.

"That is a very special cat you have, young man," said the director regaining his composure. "You must take better care of it.

"Now, as a token of our appreciation, we have something special for both of you."

With that, he opened a box and removed two medals on ribbons. The bigger one he put around Daniel's neck and the smaller one he put around Boing-Boing's neck.

"You are both now honorary members of the museum for life," said the director as he shook Daniel's hand.

"Thank you very much," responded Daniel with a big smile.

The director then reached down to shake the cat's paw and accidentally rubbed the cat's nose.

The bionic cat looked up at him and said, "Boing-Boing."

The director replied, "Little fellow, that's the nicest 'thank you' I've ever had.

"Now, young man, is there anything else you would like to say?" asked the director.

"Yes," replied Daniel, "I think I know why Boing-Boing was able to catch the jewel thief."

"Why?" asked one of the reporters.

"Because he was a cat burglar!" answered Daniel, laughing.

THE END

Maybe yes and maybe no …
… only time will tell!

Glossary

ALLERGY: A highly sensitive reaction of the body to substances like food or plant pollen or cat fur.

BATTERY: A portable device for storing and supplying electricity.

BIO: Indicates life or living organisms.

BIOENGINEERING: The design, development and use of materials and devices to help patients. Also to use engineering principles and methods to modify or produce biological products such as food.

BIONIC: Devices that combine electronic and biological features.

CERAMICS: Inorganic materials which are not metals. Examples include glass, pottery and bricks.

COMPUTER: An electronic machine which can be programmed to store information, solve problems and control machinery or electronic devices.

DIAMOND: A 'precious stone' that is made of carbon that has been highly compressed and naturally crystallised.

ELECTRICITY: A form of power or energy used for lighting, heating, working machinery or running computers.

ELECTRIC HEATER: A ceramic or metal heating element which gets hot when powered by electricity.

ELECTRONICS: Devices which can process, store and use electrical signals. Computers, TV sets, automatic washing machines operate with electronic devices.

ENGINEERING: The application of scientific principles to design, build and maintain mechanical, chemical or electrical devices or structures.

FIBRE OPTICS: Long, thin, flexible strands of glass or polymers that transmit light (photons) with very little loss of intensity. Used for communications and lighting.

GEM: A precious stone that has been cut and polished for use as jewelry.

MICROPROCESSOR: An electronic device that stores and manipulates information, such as numbers or words.

PIEZOELECTRIC CERAMICS: Special materials that generate electricity when squeezed or stretched. Conversely, materials that elongate or compress when a voltage is applied.

PROGRAM: A set of instructions for a computer.

PUPILS (IN EYES): The small round opening in the middle of your eye, that looks black and which can grow larger to let more light in or get smaller to keep light out.

ROBOT: A machine, usually controlled by a computer or microprocessor, that acts like a living being, such as a human or a cat. (**Robotics** is the use of robots to perform tasks.)

RUBY: A 'precious stone' made of aluminium oxide (corundum) and deep red in colour.

SAPPHIRE: A 'precious stone' also made of aluminium oxide, like the ruby, but deep blue in colour.

SENSOR: A mechanical, chemical or electrical device that receives and responds to an external stimulus. Our eyes are sensors that respond to light. Our ears are sensors that respond to sound. Our tongue has sensors that respond to taste.

SOLAR CELL: An electronic device that converts the energy of sunlight (photons) into electrical energy.

SUPER COMPUTER: A computer that is able to store thousands of times more information and work thousands of times faster than a normal computer.

VOICE BOX: The part of the throat of a person or a cat that allows speaking, meowing, singing, roaring and other noises. Sometimes called the larynx.

VOICE SIMULATOR: An electronic voice that makes sounds controlled by a computer or microprocessor.

VOLTS: A unit of stored electrical potential.

IF THERE ARE OTHER WORDS in this Boing-Boing adventure that you do not know try looking them up in a dictionary. Or alternately write to Professor George at professor.george@boing-boing.org for a definition.

About the Author

Larry L. Hench, Ph.D., is currently Professor of Ceramic Materials at Imperial College, London and co-director of the Imperial College Tissue Engineering and Regenerative Medicine Centre. He also served as Professor of Material Science and Engineering for 32 years at The University of Florida. He is a member of the U.S. National Academy of Engineering.

A world-renowned scientist, graduate of The Ohio State University, and Fellow of The American Ceramic Society and the Royal Society of Chemistry —Hench's numerous achievements, honours, scholarly writings, and patents, over his 40-year career, span several fields; including: ceramics, glass and glass-ceramic materials, radiation damage, nuclear waste solidification, advanced optical materials, origins of life, ethics, technology transfer, bioceramics science and clinical applications.

He is credited with the discovery of Bioglass®, the first man-made material to bond to living bone—helping millions of people; and he continues to discover new applications in bioceramics for this amazing material.

His children's books extend his love of teaching, and science and engineering to a new generation. Everything built into the stories is scientifically valid and could be done. The inspiration for these books comes from his grandchildren.

Hench, an Ohio native, now divides his time between Hampshire, England and Florida in the United States. He and his wife, June Wilson, share four children and nine grandchildren.

About the illustrator

Ruth Denise Lear was born in Wilmslow, Cheshire, England in 1965, and lives now with her husband and three children in a rural village on the outskirts of Macclesfield, Cheshire.

Her love of drawing began in childhood and has never left her. She studied at Macclesfield College and has produced and sold paintings, cards, and etchings. Her favourite media are watercolour and ink, which have been used for the Boing-Boing series.

Boing-Boing the Bionic Cat was her first book, and she couldn't have been more excited about it. Ruth says, "It is particularly apt that it should be about a cat, as I've always loved them very much–both wild and domestic; although I've never seen a bionic cat!" Not until now, anyway.

"This second book has been quite exciting for me, as Daniel and Boing-Boing meet such a wide range of creatures in the story, many of which I have never had the pleasure of drawing before!"

We think you will enjoy them!

More information on both Larry and Ruth can be found on Boing-Boing's web site: www.boing-boing.org.

The Further Adventures of Boing-Boing

Boing-Boing the Bionic Cat and the Lion's Claws continues the adventures of Daniel and Boing-Boing the Bionic Cat, the amazing, robotic cat made for him by his kindly neighbour Professor George.

In the adventure just completed Professor George programmed Boing-Boing to "ROAR" like a lion! a new feature that helped Boing-Boing tackle the jewel thief. In this next adventure this feature and some special new technology prove helpful in the London Zoo.

What excitement awaits the invincible duo, Daniel and his bionic cat, during their trip to the London Zoo? Snakes? Elephants? Monkeys? A fierce Lion? During an afternoon trip to the zoo, Daniel and Boing-Boing meet Daniel's friend Amy and 'fall' into an adventure which pits them against one of the fiercest forces in the animal kingdom.

Professor George, Boing-Boing, and Daniel bring engineering and science to life through the creation of a bionic cat and their exciting adventures and discoveries. This third book in the Boing-Boing the Bionic Cat series continues to entertain while teaching children about the evolving process of science, the benefits and limits of technology, and the caring and understanding from adult role models.

To read the first chapter of Boing-Boing's next adventure visit: www.boing-boing.org.

www.boing-boing.org

Find out more about Boing-Boing, Danny, Professor George and friends at Boing-Boing's web site.

Online you will find:
- Games
- Competitions
- Puzzles
- How to make your own bionic cat

And much, much more.

Kitty-Kits

Take a break, make a kit-kat.

Explore the world of robotic engineering with your very own Boing-Boing the Bionic Cat Kitty-Kits.

For more information visit Professor George's workshop at: www.boing-boing.org/workshop or follow the links from the home page.

Teachers and Schools

Boing-Boing is not just a house cat, you can find Boing-Boing in schools as well as part of a new cross-curriculum teaching scheme for seven year olds and up.

The objective of this scheme is to enhance the interest of primary school children, boys and girls, in the sciences, engineering and technology, and maintain that interest throughout their school years.

If you would like more information on this scheme, and to find out what teachers and schools think about Boing-Boing, please call the publisher or visit the Boing-Boing web site at: www.boing-boing.org.